BLACK VODKA

BLACK VODKA

TEN STORIES

Deborah Levy

BLOOMSBURY

NEW YORK · LONDON · NEW DELHI · SYDNEY

Published by Bloomsbury USA, New York
Bloomsbury is a trademark of Bloomsbury Publishing Plc

"Vienna" and "Stardust Nation" were first published in *Ambit*; "Cave Girl" in *Here Lies* (Trip Street Press, 2001); "Roma" in *Vertigo* magazine; "Black Vodka" in *Road Stories* (Royal Borough of Kensington and Chelsea, 2012). "Shining a Light" was commissioned for an installation by the Wapping Project. "Placing a Call" was commissioned by Margarita Production for the narrative project *Loose Promise*, a collaboration with performer Kate McIntosh. "Vienna," "Pillow Talk," "Simon Tegala's Heart in 13 Parts," "A Better Way to Live," and "Cave Girl" were published together in *Pillow Talk in Europe and Other Places* (Dalkey Archive Press, 2003).

All papers used by Bloomsbury USA are natural, recyclable products made from wood grown in well-managed forests. The manufacturing processes conform to the environmental regulations of the country of origin.

LIBRARY OF CONGRESS CATALOGING-IN-PUBLICATION DATA HAS BEEN APPLIED FOR

ISBN: 978-1- 62040-672-4

First published in Great Britain in 2013 by & Other Stories
First U.S. edition 2014

1 3 5 7 9 10 8 6 4 2

Printed and bound in the U.S.A. by Thomson-Shore Inc., Dexter, Michigan

Bloomsbury books may be purchased for business or promotional use. For information on bulk purchases please contact Macmillan Corporate and Premium Sales Department at specialmarkets@macmillan.com.

CONTENTS

BLACK VODKA

The first time I met Lisa I knew she was going to help me become a very different sort of man. Knowing this felt like a summer holiday. It made me relax – and I am quite a tense person. There is something you should know about me. I have a little hump on my back, a mound between my shoulder blades. You will notice when I wear a shirt without a jacket that there is more to me than first meets the eye. It's strange how fascinating human beings find both celebrity and deformity in their own species. People sink their eyes into my hump for six seconds longer than proto-col should allow, and try to work out the difference between themselves and me. The boys called me 'Ali' at school because that's what they thought camels were called. Ali Ali Ali. Ali's got the hump. The word 'playground' does not really provide an accurate sense of the sort of ethnic cleansing that went on behind the gates that were supposed to keep us safe.

I was instructed in the art of Not Belonging from a very tender age. Deformed. Different. Strange. Go Ho-me Ali, Go Ho-me. In fact I was born in Southend-on-Sea, and so were those boys, but I was exiled to the Arabian Desert and not allowed to smoke with them behind the cockle sheds.

There is something else you ought to know about me. I write copy for a leading advertising agency. I earn a lot of money and my colleagues reluctantly respect me because they suspect I'm less content than they are. I have made it my professional business to understand that no one respects ruddy-faced happiness.

I first glimpsed Lisa at the presentation launch for the naming and branding of a new vodka. My agency had won the account for the advertising campaign and I was standing on a small raised stage pointing to a slide of a starry night sky. I adjusted my mic clip and began.

   'Black Vodka . . . ' I said, slightly sinisterly, 'vodka *Noir*, will appeal to those in need of stylish angst. As Victor Hugo might have put it, we are alone, bereft, and the night falls upon us; to drink Black Vodka is to be in mourning for our lives.'

I explained that vodka was mostly associated with the communist countries of the former Eastern bloc, where it was well known that the exploration of abstract, subjective and conceptual ideas in these regimes was the ultimate defiance of the individual against the state. Black Vodka would hitch a nostalgic ride on all of this and be sold as the edgy choice for the cultured and discerning.

My colleagues sipped their lattes (the intern had done a Starbucks run) and listened carefully to my angle. When I insisted that Vodka Noir had high cheekbones, a few of the guys laughed uneasily. I am known in the office as the Crippled Poet. Then I noticed someone sitting in the audience, a woman with long brown hair (very blond at the ends) who was not from the agency. She had her arms folded across her grey cashmere sweater; an open notebook lay on her lap. Now and again she'd pick it up and doodle with her pencil. My sharp eyes (long sight) confirmed that this stranger in our small community was observing me rather clinically.

•

After the presentation, my colleague Richard introduced me to the woman with the notebook. Although
he did not say so, I assumed she was his new girlfriend. Richard is known for splashing his footballer's
body with a heady cologne every morning. 'West
Indian Limes'. Its effect on me is both arousing and
desperately melancholy. I could buy five bottles of
that seductive cologne tomorrow, yet to draw attention to my damaged body in this way would be to
underline its difference from Richard's. Anyway, it
was quite a shock to see him with the woman whose
clinical gaze had for some mysterious reason awoken
in me the kind of nihilistic lust I was attempting to
whip up in my Vodka Noir campaign.

Richard smiled affectionately at me, apparently
amused at something he couldn't be bothered to
explain.

'Lisa is an archaeologist. I thought she'd be
interested in your presentation.'

Her eyes were pale blue.

'Would you buy Black Vodka, Lisa?'

She told me she would, yes, she would give it
a go, and then she screamed because Richard had
crept up behind her and his hands were clasping her
narrow waist like a handcuff.

•

As I put away my laptop, I felt an unwelcome blast of anger. I think I suddenly wanted more than anything else to be a man without a burden on his back. After a presentation we tend to open champagne and instruct the interns to order in snacks. But when I saw a tray of sun-dried tomatoes arranged on tiny, pesto-filled pastry cases, I wanted to punch them onto the floor.

I left the office early. I even left without asking my boss what he thought of my presentation. Tom Mines is the Cruel Man of the agency (though he would call his cruelty 'insight') and he suffers from livid eczema on his wrists and hands. For as long as I've known him, he's always bought jackets with extra-long sleeves. For obvious reasons, I am fascinated by how other people conceal their physical suffering.

I muttered something about being summoned to an emergency and left quickly before Tom could point out that the emergency was me. But I did not leave before walking straight over to Lisa, aware that Tom Mines had his eye on me, his thin grey fingers twisted around the cuffs of his jacket. What I did next might sound strange: I gave Richard's girlfriend my card. The surprise she attempted to express with her facial muscles, her raised eyebrows, her mocking lips slightly parted, was really not that convincing because of what I knew. When Lisa was doodling in her notebook, she had let it rest open on her lap. From my position on the raised stage, I could see quite clearly that she had drawn a sketch of me on the left-hand page. A picture of a naked, hunchbacked man, with every single organ of his body labelled. Underneath her rather too accurate portrait (should I be flattered that she imagined me naked?) she'd scribbled two words: *Homo sapiens*.

She called me. Lisa actually pressed the digits that connected her to my voice. I asked her straight away if she'd like to join me for supper on Friday? No, she can't make Friday. It is usual for people attracted to each other to pretend they have full and busy lives but I have an incredible facility to wade through human shame with no shoes on. I told her if she couldn't make Friday, I was free on Monday, Tuesday, Wednesday and Thursday and that the weekend looked hopeful too.

We agreed to meet on Wednesday in South Kensington. She said she liked the big sky in that part of town and I suggested we drink our way through the vast menu of flavoured vodkas at the Polish Club, not far from the Royal Albert Hall. This way we could conduct a bit of field research for my Vodka Noir concept. She said she was more than happy to be my assistant.

That night I dreamt (again) of Poland. In this recurring dream I am in Warsaw on a train to Southend-on-Sea. There is a soldier in my carriage. He kisses his mother's hand and then he kisses his girlfriend's lips. I am watching him in the old mirror attached to the wall of our carriage and I can see he has a humped back under his khaki uniform. When I wake up there are always tears on my cheeks, transparent as vodka but warm as rain.

There's something about rain that makes me slam the doors of cabs extra hard. I love the rain. It heightens every gesture, injects it with 5ml of unspecific yearning. On Wednesday night it was raining when the cab dropped me off on the Exhibition Road in London's Zone 1. In the distance I could see autumn leaves on the tall trees in Hyde Park. The air was soft and cool. As I began to walk up Exhibition Road, I knew that under the twenty-first-century paving stones there had once been fields and market gardens. I wanted to laze in those fields with Lisa stretched across my lap, the clouds unfolding above us, and I wanted the schoolboys who told me I was a freak to want to be me.

I walked deliberately slowly up to the white Georgian town house that is the Polish Club. The building was donated to the Polish resistance during the Second World War, later becoming a cultural meeting place, a kind of home to those who could not return to a Poland ruled by Stalin. While researching the Black Vodka concept, I had discovered that, like myself, Stalin was physically misshapen. His face was pitted from the smallpox, one of his arms was longer than the other, he was called 'tiger' because his eyes were yellow and he was short enough to have to wear platform shoes. I have never worn shoes with heels to make me feel bolder, but I have always thought of myself as lost property, someone waiting to be claimed. To be offered an elegant home for a few hours at the hospitable Polish Club always does good things for my dignity.

I hung my coat on a wooden hanger, placed it on the clothes rail in the foyer and made my way into the bar, where a polite and serene waitress from Lublin confirmed my booking in the dining room. She discreetly invited me to 'enjoy a drink until my companion arrives'. Keen to obey her, I ordered a double shot of pepper vodka. Thirty minutes later, I had researched the raspberry, honey, caraway, plum and apple vodkas, and my companion had still not arrived. The sky was darkening outside the window. An elderly woman in a green felt hat sat on the velvet chair next to me, scribbling some sort of mathematical equation on a scrap of paper. She was so lost in thought, I began to worry that somewhere else in the world, another mathematician would pick up on those thoughts and at this very moment, 8.25pm, find a strategy to solve the equation before she did. It was possible that while she sat in her chair struggling with the endless zeros that seemed to perplex her deeply, someone else would be standing on a stage in São Paulo or Ljubljana, collecting a fat cheque for their contribution to human knowledge. Would I, too, be waiting in endless humiliation for Lisa, who was probably at this moment lying in Richard's arms while he kissed the zero of her mouth?

No I would not. She arrived, late and breathless, and I could see she was genuinely sorry to have kept me waiting. I ordered her the cherry vodka while she told me the reason she was late was that she had been planning a dig that was soon to take place in Cornwall, but the computer had crashed and she'd lost most of her data.

There is nothing that feels as good as breathing near someone you desire. The past of my youth was not a good place to be. Is it strange then, that I am attracted to a woman who is obsessed with digging up the past? Lisa and I are sitting in the dining room of the Polish Club on our first date. We arrange the starched linen napkins over our laps, admire the chandelier above our heads and discuss the oily black eggs, the caviar that comes from the beluga, osietra and sevruga varieties of sturgeon. The waitress from Lublin takes our order and Lisa, naturally, wants to know less about fish and more about me.

'So where do you live?' She asks me this as if I am an exotic find that she is required to label in black Indian ink.

I tell her I own a three-bedroom flat with a west-facing balcony in a Victorian double-fronted villa in Notting Hill Gate. I want to bore her.

I tell her I never dream or cry or swear or shake or snack on cereal instead of apples. Better slowly to prove more interesting than I first appear.

Lisa looks bored.

I tell her that my mother wanted me to be a priest because she thought I'd look best in loose-fitting clothes.

She laughs and plays with the ends of her hair. She shuts her eyes and then opens them. She fiddles with her mobile, which she has placed on the table. Lisa shuffles her shoes, which are red and suede. She eats a hearty portion of duck with apple sauce and discovers I like delicate dumplings stuffed with mushroom because I am a vegetarian. When she stabs her fork into the meat it oozes pale red blood which she mops up with a piece of white bread; little, delicate dabs of the wrist as she brings the blood and bread up to her mouth. She eats with appetite and enjoyment. That she is a carnivore pleases me.

After a while she orders a slice of cheesecake and asks me if I was born a hunchback.

'Yes.'

'Sometimes it's difficult to tell.'

'What do you mean?'

'Well, some people have bad posture.'

'Oh.'

Lisa licks her fingers. Apparently it's an excellent cheesecake. I am pleased she is pleased. The waitress offers us a glass of liqueur from a bottle that has 'a whole Italian pear' lurking inside it. The pear is peeled. It is a naked pear. We accept and I say to Lisa, 'We should get that pear out of the bottle and make a sorbet with it' – as if that is something I do all the time. In fact I have never made sorbet. She likes that. It is as if the invitation to wedge the pear out of the bottle is like freeing a genie. She becomes more animated and talks about her job. Apparently when she finds human remains on a dig, bones for example, they have to be stored in a methodical way. Heavy bones, the long bones, are packed at the bottom of a box; lighter bones such as vertebrae are packed at the top.

'Archaeology is an approach to uncovering the past,' she tells me, sipping her liqueur – which, strangely, does not taste of pear.

'So when you go on a dig, you record and inter-pret the physical remains of the past, is that right?'

'Sort of. I like to know how people used to live and what their habits were.'

'You dig up their beliefs and culture.'

'Well you can't dig up a belief,' she says. 'But the material culture, the objects and artefacts that people leave behind, will give me clues to their beliefs.'

'I see. You know why I like you, Lisa?'

'Why do you like me?'

'Because I think you see me as an archaeological site.'

'I am a bit of an explorer,' she says. 'I'd like to see the bone that protrudes in your thoracic spine.'

At that moment I drop the silver fork in my right hand. It falls noiselessly to the carpet and bounces before it falls again. I bend down to pick it up and because I am nervous and have downed too much vodka, I start to go on an archaeological dig of my own. In my mind I lift up the faded rose-pink carpet of the Polish Club in South Kensington and find underneath it a forest full of wild mushrooms and swooping bats that live upside down. This is a Polish forest covered in new snow in the murderous twentieth century. At the same time, in the first decade of the twenty-first, I can see the feet of customers eating herrings with sour cream two metres away from my own table. Their shoes are made from suede and leather. A grey wolf prowls this dark forest, its ears alert to the sound of spoons stirring chocolate-dusted cappuccinos in West London. When it starts to dig up an unnamed grave that has just been filled with soil, I do not wish to continue with this mental excavation, so I pick up the fork and nod at Lisa, who has been gazing at the lump on my back as if staring through the lens of a microscope.

The rain tonight is horizontal. It makes me feel reckless. I want to give in to its force. As we step onto Exhibition Road I slip my arm around Lisa's shoulders and she does not grimace. Her hair is soaking wet and so are her red suede shoes.

'I am going home,' she tells me. She beckons to a vacant taxi on the other side of the road and all the time the warm rain falls upon us like the tears in my dream. Her voice is gentle. Rain does that to voices. It makes them intimate and suggestive. While the taxi does a U-turn she stands behind me and presses her hands into my hump as if she is listening to it breathe. And then she takes her forefinger and traces around it, getting an exact sense of its shape. It's the kind of thing cops do to a corpse with a piece of chalk. Now Lisa bends down and opens the door of the taxi. As she slides her long legs into the back seat, she shouts her destination to the driver.

'Tower Bridge.'

He nods and adjusts the meter.

When she smiles I can see her sharp white teeth.

'Look, you know that Richard is my boyfriend – but why don't you come home with me and compare notes on those vodkas?'

I don't need any persuading. I jump in beside her and slam the door extra hard. As the cab pulls out, Lisa leans forwards and starts to kiss me. Does she want to know more about my habits and beliefs and how I live? Or is she curious to find out if her sketch of Homo sapiens was an accurate representation of my body?

The meter is going berserk like my heartbeat while the moon drifts over the wildlife gardens of the Natural History Museum. Somewhere inside it, pressed under glass, are twelve ghost moths (Hepialus humuli), of earliest evolutionary lineage. These ghosts once flew in pastures, dropped their eggs to the ground and slept through the day. There is so much of the world to record and classify, it's hard to know how to find a language for it. So I am going to start exactly where I am now. Life is beautiful! Vodka is black! Pears are naked! Rain is horizontal! Moths are ghosts. Only some of this is true, but you should know that this does not scare me as much as the promise of love.

SHINING A LIGHT

It is the last Saturday in August. Alice is waiting in baggage reclaim at Prague airport, and she knows before it is completely certain that her bag will not appear. For twenty minutes the luggage belt has looped along its tracks in a slow mesmerising circle, a dead grey river. Her bag is not on it. Yes, she can fill in a form. She can give the official her mobile number and the address of her hotel near Malá Strana, but she tells herself to accept that she has lost everything. The cheerfully vague official in charge of missing luggage (her name is Petra) understands that filling in the form is a waste of both their time but she takes the trouble to guide Alice through the procedure. Petra's breath smells of aniseed or something like that. Alice isn't really bothering; she can barely read her own hurried writing. The worst thing is that her mobile-phone charger is in the bag that has gone missing. Even if the airline does find it and calls her to collect it, her phone will be out of charge.

Petra has a system in place to process loss – and she has other information too. She warns Alice about dishonest cab drivers; the minibus shuttle will drive her to her destination for a cheaper price than a private cab. Also, given that Alice has lost her bag with her mobile charger in it, she should use a public telephone box and buy a phone card. The emergency number is 112. And then she tells her there will be a screening of a film in the park on Tuesday night. It's free but everyone dresses up.

It is Tuesday night and Alice is dancing in a park in central Prague in the blue dress she has worn for three days.

The film Petra referred to turns out to be an outdoor screening of Martin Scorsese's documentary of the Rolling Stones in concert. Midges are biting her arms, it is eleven at night and the moon is shining on the crowd. Two Serbian women, Jasna and Adrijana, dance with her while Mick Jagger sings 'Yeah, you light up my life'. Alice has only just met them but she is pleased to have their company. She tells Jasna that when Mick walks away from the microphone to change his costume, the stage goes dead because he is not on it. Like the luggage belt at the airport when she realised her bag was not there.

Jasna's and Adrijana's boyfriends are queuing for beers. They wave to a man selling frankfurters and shout, 'Hot dogs!' Adrijana insists on buying one for Alice too. They smother the hot dogs in ketchup and drink beer and watch the swans sleeping on the black water of the Vltava. When the film ends they all invite Alice to join them for a swim the next day in a lake just outside Prague. Apparently it's not really a lake, it's an old mine that flooded a few years ago in a rainstorm. It's near a cornfield and there are castles nearby and a forest and eagles. Would she like to go? Alice nods and smiles and they all cheer and wave their beer bottles at the dark sky.

Later, when she walks over the cobblestones towards her hotel in Malá Strana she realises that arriving in a country with nothing but the clothes she is wearing has made her more reckless, but more introspective too.

The car that pulls up outside her hotel on Wednesday afternoon is a beaten-up Mercedes. Adrijana shares the Merc with three other families and Wednesday is her driving day. Jasna, Petar and Dimitar, who are sitting in the back, move up to make room for Alice to squeeze in. There is someone else in the car too. He is introduced to Alice as a famous brilliant terrific genius composer of electronic music. The composer tells her his name is Alex but she can call him Mr Composer if she likes. And then he doesn't say a word for the entire journey.

When they finally arrive at the lake that was once a mine, the green water is still and flat. Alice thinks it might have some sort of force that will suck her deep into the earth and make her disappear like her lost suitcase. Jasna lends her a swimming costume but Alice takes her time getting changed. She folds her blue dress carefully and then places it on a rock. Everyone is in the water, except for Mr Composer who refuses to swim and sits on the same rock as her dress, buttoning up his jacket and shivering. When he catches Alice's eye he shrugs his shoulders and wryly translates the sign at the entrance to the lake. He tells her it says, 'DANGER! NO SWIMMING!' He watches her climb down the clay path and dive into the water. It is very cold and she cannot feel her legs. Adrijana and Jasna have swum out to the centre of the lake where it is deepest. They have pinned up their brown hair and swim calmly and slowly together like the swans on the Vltava. After a while they turn on their backs and stare at the sky.

Alice climbs out of the water and sits dripping wet next to Mr Composer or Alex or whoever he is. He hands her a plastic carrier bag. Inside it is a heavy square of cake. He explains that it is baklava made by his mother who he has just returned from visiting in Belgrade. It is not like the baklava Alice is used to because it's heavy like bread. He takes out his mobile and Alice hears him say, 'I'm at a lake outside Prague with Alice who is from Britain, which is why I am speaking to you in English. She wants me to tell you she likes your cake.'

When he ends the call, Alice points out he has the same mobile phone as she does. That's really interesting Alice, he says, and tells her that he, like Adrijana and Jasna, had to cross three borders 'during the war' to get to Prague. Every now and again she notices a strained look in his eyes. She is just about to ask him something when Jasna creeps up behind her holding out her blue dress like a flag. It has fallen off the rock and is smeared with mud.

On the way back to Prague they stop at a pub for beer and Alex orders a plate of smoked ham. While the others are talking he tells Alice that though they are all from Serbia they did not know each other in their own country. They met for the first time in Prague. In fact, he says, we didn't really want to meet each other at first because you never know what each other is going to be like. Adrijana asks Alice if she has heard of a famous European philosopher. She tells her the philosopher's name. Alice has never heard of him. Well, he has this beautiful wife, Adrijana says to Alice. Beautiful like you. Long blond hair. But this philosopher, who we like very much because he has written about what life is like for us, he is very, very busy. Always giving lectures all over the world. In fact right now he is probably writing a lecture somewhere and it is midnight and the philosopher's beautiful wife is on the phone and she is saying to her husband, so kiss yourself good night tonight and I will kiss myself good night and you stroke your own hair tonight and I will stroke my own arm tonight. Alice does not really understand why they are all laughing so much. She feels lonely and out of the loop, whatever the loop is, and anyway she's not that sure the loop is a good place to be.

'Are you ok, Alice?' Alex prods her arm with his long fingers. 'By the way,' he says, 'I really like your blue dress.' He asks her when she is returning to the UK. She tells him she is leaving later that evening. 'Uh huh,' he says. 'Then tonight you will kiss yourself good night. And I will kiss myself good night.' He tells her he's going for a walk in the woods to stretch his legs before the drive back to Prague. The woods are just across the road from the pub. Alice asks if he minds if she joins him? She wants to see autumn leaves.

The sky has clouded by the time they cross the road to where the entrance to the woods begins. When they get there, Alice doesn't want to walk with him after all. She has changed her mind. He says, 'Well, anyway, I'm really happy to meet you.' He waves his hands around a bit and suddenly grabs the ends of her blond hair with his fingertips. She wants to ask him where on the map his country is but it sounds insulting and ignorant and she doesn't think she can ask a question like that. He lets go of her hair and he says, 'I really like so much your blue dress and red tights. If I stop working in my stupid job, one day I will buy you a pair of shoes.' And then he walks into the woods.

The season is turning and she wants to go home to England. A bird scrambles in the upper branches of a tree. She watches the bird and she thinks about Adrijana and Jasna swimming in the deep, cold lake. They have been hurt in ways she has not been hurt. They have left all the seasons in their country behind them.

When she looks at her watch she wonders if Alex might have got lost. Has something happened to him in the wood? She thinks something is about to happen. This is how she felt at the baggage reclaim. A feeling of dread in her stomach when she knew her bag had gone missing. Strange thoughts occur to her now as she waits for him. She wonders if there are people hiding in the woods because they have lost their country and their home and their children and their sister and cousin and she thinks Alex might have lost his brother and father because of something he said earlier. She thinks about the form she had to fill in at the airport and the official who looked bored when she listed all the things she had lost.

The material of her blue dress is rubbing against her skin as she paces up and down the road on the edge of the woods. A wind suddenly blows in and then she sees him.

He is walking towards her. There are small leaves in his hair as he stands too close and tells her his name is not Alex. Not exactly. It is Aleksandar. He tells her he saw a deer in the woods with small antlers and how he used to have an Italian coffee-making machine in his kitchen in his country which he liked a lot, the coffee machine he means, not the country, and he is sorry to have missed the Rolling Stones film last night in the park because then he would have been near her a little bit longer. Aleksandar squeezes his lips and lowers his eyes. He offers to charge up her mobile phone for her before she leaves for London. He folds his arms across his chest and leans back on his heels as if to get a better view of her and then he tells her it's nice to watch her laughing at him while the wind blows her hair about.

VIENNA

'Before I forget,' Magret's voice is low and vague, 'I want to test my new microwave.'

He nods, as if he is a secretary taking notes from an inscrutable Executive Director who wears purple lipstick to frighten the more timid of her staff. She rips the silver foil from a carton of langoustines and slides them into the microwave that still has the price taped to its side. He watches her bend her long neck to check the minutes and seconds and then fold her arms against the pearl-grey cashmere that hugs her small breasts. While she waits she tells him she has no idea why her husband has bought her a microwave.

When the timer pings she takes out the langoustines and places them in front of him in a delicate blue china bowl. He cracks the pink and grey shells with his fingers and then sucks the white flesh into his mouth, suddenly aware that her accent, which he can't place, makes him think of wolves. He looks down at the frayed cuffs of his shirt sleeves and notices a small rash on the back of both his hands. Does she know he has brought his agitation and turbulence into the white walls of her apartment? The rash on his hands is the memory of saying goodbye to his small children when he left the family house, knowing he was never going to return.

Magret walks across the carpet towards a sleek black answering machine and presses the Play button. A man's voice speaks to her. He suspects it is the authoritarian voice of her new Italian husband.

>*Ti penso sempre*
>*Mi manchi*
>*Cara mia, ti voglio bene*

'What does it mean?' He understands that her husband has told her he loves her but wants her to tell him anyway.

'It means now I am going to pull down the blinds and you and I are going to take off our clothes.'

For the first time all evening he feels frightened. He wraps his fingers around the pulse of his wrist and shuts his eyes. A boiler concealed somewhere in the building makes the sing-song sound of cicadas. Worst of all, a picture of his ex-wife slides into his head when he least wants it to. She is sitting with his daughter and baby son, threading glass beads onto a length of red string.

When he opens his eyes, Magret is naked. Her long limbs are warm, he discovers, moving his cold hand between her legs and leaving it there, letting her move his fingers, while the hidden boiler fills the room with its own peculiar sounds. He likes her disdain for small talk after sex, relieved she does not ask him to exchange small confidences, pleased not to have to tell her about his wife and children, temporary bedsit and unpacked suitcase.

But he doesn't want to let go of her yet.

He asks her a question in the language of his father, a language he has almost forgotten how to speak.

'I don't know what you're saying.' She sits up and shakes down her hair.

'It's Russian for do you have children?'

'I do not.'

Now he knows she does not have children. This is one of the few things he knows about her. He knows she does not need him. He knows she can cook langoustines to perfection in a brand new microwave. He knows she is married. That is all he knows.

She stands up and walks to a cupboard made from Swedish blond wood, aware that he is watching her take down a blue silk bath robe and loop it over her long, tanned arms.

She is middle Europe, he thinks. She is Vienna. She is Austria. She is a silver teaspoon. She is cream. She is schnapps. She is strudel dusted with white icing sugar. She is the sound of polite applause. She is a chandelier. She is a velvet curtain. She is made from the horn of deer found deep in the pine forests of middle Europe. She is spun from money. She smells of burnt sugar. She is snow. She is fur. She is leather. She is gold. She is someone else's property. He holds out his arms, inviting her back to her own bed, inviting middle Europe to share her wealth, to let him steal some of her silver, to

let him make footprints across her snow and drink
her schnapps.

Magret ignores his invitation to return to his thin
white arms.

'My husband wants me to learn Italian. So he
tests me on the seasons. I have to say in perfect Italian
all the months, January, February, March, until I get
to December and then he corrects my accent.'

'But you speak Italian don't you?'

He hides his hands under the sheet, hands that
are livid and itching.

'Not well enough for my husband.'

He realises he does not know where she is from
or if she works or why she lets him have sex with her.

'What is your first language?'

'There are so many languages.' She flicks an
invisible light switch and the room fills with unwelcome white strobe.

'I am going to swim in the pool downstairs.'

He nods. He has been dismissed by middle Europe,
who has plans that do not include him in the structure of her day. Again, he feels foolish, not sure what

it is he wants from her or why he feels so excited when she calls him to say she is in town. He climbs out of bed and looks for his clothes. While he puts on his trousers, shirt, cufflinks and jacket, she slips on a modest white swimming costume. They do not speak until he is standing on the marble floor outside her front door. Only then, facing him in his suit and the heavy overcoat he bought in Zurich when he knew his marriage was over, barefoot in her Italian swimming costume, does she attempt to say goodbye.

Gute Nacht.
  Spokojnoj nochi, Magret.

As he walks to the tube station he thinks about the snow of his childhood and all the trams he rode on with his sister. He thinks about the wars and famines his parents lived through and about the 11:07 that leaves promptly every Sunday morning from Zurich where his ex-wife and children live. He thinks about Magret swimming in the cold pool below her apartment, her head surfacing, her mouth opening to take a breath. He knows she is dead inside and he is aroused that this is so, and he takes out a cigarette and lights it. He thinks about how there is life with rye bread and black tea and there is life with champagne and wild salmon. He can live without champagne but he cannot live without his children; that is a grief he knows he cannot endure but he must endure and he knows his hands will itch for ever. He thinks about feeling used, teased, abused and mocked by middle Europe, whose legs were wrapped around his appallingly grateful body ten minutes ago, and he thinks about the twentieth century that ended at the same time as his marriage.

STARDUST NATION

Good morning.

The London dawn. The light. The birds. The car alarms. The agitated men and women waiting for buses that don't arrive. Does anyone still say 'Good morning' in the breezy manner of 1950s black-and-white English films? When I was five years old my mother employed a Dutch tutor to teach me mathematics and biology. She definitely had a breezy morning manner when she walked into the nursery in her high white leather shoes.

'*Goedemorgen*, little Thomas! How is your heart-beat today?'

Children of my class were taught always to answer an adult politely (no matter what they said or did to you) so I would reply, 'My heartbeat is very good today, thank you.'

One day I detoured from my usual reply and told her the truth.

'My heartbeat is jumping all over the place, *danke*.'

She was touched by my attempt at her language and insisted I wash my hands three times before presenting me with a sweet Dutch milk pudding called *vla*.

But *vla* is not what I want to tell you about. Not at all.

Although I am sitting on the edge of the bed in my West London apartment sipping cognac from an eggcup (well, it is breakfast after all), my mind is very much elsewhere. Let me describe the sequence of events so far. We will have to spin time backwards to seven months ago. A cross on my agency calendar (a gift to our clients) marks the precise date, 9th August 2004, when my colleague Nick Gazidis telephoned me at 2am from a howling beach in southern Spain, weeping broken words and images into my ear.

'We are stardust, Tom.'

'Nick? Where are you?'

'Flamingos. Salt hills.'
'Where are you phoning from?'
'The moon.'

I knew Nick was on holiday in Almería because I
am his boss and have to approve his dates. I seem
to remember they filmed *Lawrence of Arabia* on the
sand dunes in that desolate part of Spain. When I
looked up Almería in my guidebook it was described
as 'a lunar landscape', so perhaps he hadn't gone
completely nuts after all. Over the years, I have told
Nick more about my life than anyone else I know, so
it felt right to return his remarkable gift of empathy
by listening to his strange words without judgment.
He was somewhere on a beach, it was 4am his time
and he didn't know how to get back to his hotel. I
could hear him sobbing in the wind as he dropped
coins into a public telephone.

'Tom? Are you still there?'
    'Yes. I'm still here.'
    'My father beat me when I was a kid. Did you
know that?'

•

Nick's full name is Nikos Gazidis. His father, Mr Gazidis, is a gentle, elderly man who owns a drycleaner's in Kentish Town and has never beaten anyone in his life. I've met him twice, both times bent over his sewing machine, a tape measure draped over his shoulders. Mr Gazidis is awed by the money his son earns at my agency and treats him like a god. So you can imagine how I brooded on Nick's peculiar phone call.

My father was a lieutenant colonel in the British Army. Uncomfortable with the lack of excitement on home leave, he did tend to start small post-traumatic wars against his eight-year-old son, usually with his leather belt. While he beat me, I used to imagine myself somewhere else, often on the moon, a boy astronaut floating head over heels away from Lt-Col Banbury-Mines, away from my forlorn mother, away from the marmalade jar and toast rack on the break-fast table, away from the thank yous and yes pleases people seem so nostalgic for these days. My Dutch tutor was appalled by my father and taught me a few martial arts moves specially designed to throw a grown man to the ground.

I had of course told Nick about my childhood over the years, usually in the pub after work. On these occasions he took off his tie while he listened. A little streak of eczema always crept into his right cheek afterwards. I too have long blazed with eczema, especially on my wrists.

Three days later, when Nick returned to work, he wore a Paul Smith suit like the rest of us and acted as if nothing out of the ordinary had happened.

'How are you, Nick?'

'Yeah. Um. Sorry about that. I'm fine.'

For a man who had so recently been deranged he gave the impression of being entirely normal. I too have spent much of my life perfecting this performance. Nick is a promising accountant and I have been his encouraging mentor. So I kept one eye on him when I invited him to join my copywriters and take a look at a PowerPoint projection of the English meadows I played in as a boy. We were about to launch a shampoo that would conquer the bathrooms of the nation. I proposed we call the shampoo MEADOW MILK.

'Milk,' I suggested, 'is an opaque white fluid secreted by female mammals for the nourishment of their young. It is the elixir of life itself.'

I glanced at Nick. Tears were spilling down his face and his hands hung limply by his side like the dead pheasants my father brought home from the meadow. Afterwards, over a glass of champagne, he told me the reason for his embarrassed tears.

'My Dutch tutor used milk to make me custard pudding after my father hit out at me. And the meadow you showed in your slide . . . I used to hide from him in the long grass when I was eight.'

I smiled and patted him on the back. Nick grew up in a small, Victorian terraced house in Archway, north London. I don't want to presume, but those cramped, damp houses held together with bricks and spit do not usually come with meadows attached to them. Yet I think I understood what was happening. There is a slight shamanistic edge to what we do here at the agency, which is to say that it is our job to crash into the unconscious of the consumer and broadcast a number of messages that all end with 'buy this product'. Nick had somehow extended his brief as Head of Finance – and crashed inside me. Although I had told him about hiding in that meadow, I had yet to explain why. I thought that could wait. Giving the right information at the right time is after all the art of what we do here at the agency.

•

A week later Nick called me again, as I knew he would, this time on a Sunday at 3am from his water-front apartment with river views and twenty-four-hour security. The uniformed guard who sat in his cabin all night long just outside the electronic gates obviously did not make Nick feel safe and sound.

'Tom? Um . . . I'm not feeling right.'

I caught a cab straight away, and actually wish I had not been so hasty. Nick was in boxer shorts when he opened the door. The man's chest was still tanned from Spain. A beautiful man with tears in his eyes.

'We are stardust, Tom.'

'That's what you said in Almería.'

I thought I'd better give him something to do and suggested he make us some strong black coffee. He was remarkably composed, given the circum-stances. True, his hands shook as he put the espresso pot on the gas, and I observed that his eyes flickered over the ceiling as he asked me strange questions.

'What's your name? Can you spell it for me?'

'T-h-o-m-a-s.'

Nick frowned.

'No. No. Um. I mean what's my name?'

'Your name is Nikos.'

I could see some kind of agony leak from inside Nick and fill his eyes, which were already full.

I sat at the table smoking too many cigarettes while he looked around for cups in his orderly, stainless-steel kitchen.

When Nick finally sat down he was sweating.

'I've had a very bad night, Tom.'

'How bad?'

'I keep thinking I should visit my mother. I hear her voice all the time.' He started to mimic a pinched, choking female voice. 'Devon is lovely at this time of year. We can eat crab sandwiches in that pub you appreciate in Salcombe.'

Nick's mother does not live in Devon. She lives in Kentish Town, where she is a teaching assistant at the local primary school. Needless to say, my mother does live in Salcombe and she always insists we eat a crab sandwich at the Fisherman's Arms with the other widows she has grown fond of over so many lonely years. I sit with them, the only man in their lives, a thin wreck of a man in a smart suit, while they talk about the weather and TV soaps and how appalling it is that teachers don't wear suits like mine any more. Of course my mother and I cannot talk about my childhood, so it is better to talk about the lack of English as she understands it in England. I always carry my briefcase with me on these occasions and slip outside as often as I can get away with for a gulp of cognac in the fresh air. Whenever I visit my mother I am in a right old state.

'You are in a right old state, Nick.' I patted his brown neck with my scabby hand.

'Tell me about it,' he groaned.

I was tactfully silent for a few minutes, but I was excited too. Nick had somehow made my biography his own. Rather him than me, I must say. To be honest it was a tremendous relief to see how distressed he was. I started to tell him more about that afternoon when I ran into the meadow.

'I was eight years old . . . the year Britain went decimal and John Lennon wrote 'Imagine'. The year *A Clockwork Orange* was released and I lost it with my father . . . ' I gave him a clear picture of myself as an eight-year-old boy running at my father with a kitchen knife in my hand. I told him how I was too small to take on a big army man but my tutor helped me. That is what tutors are supposed to do after all – they help their pupils. Her blond plait was tied with a white ribbon. A gold crucifix attached to a fragile gold chain glistened between her breasts. She smelt of milk and mown grass and I was her calf. After she wrestled him to the ground, her eyes told me what to do. I plunged the knife between his ribs.

And then she ran out into the meadow.

My father was lying very still on the kitchen floor.

And then my own warm urine trickled down my legs.

What if my father suddenly stood up and chased after me?

How I described it to Nick was like this:

'Imagine a butterfly displayed in a glass case suddenly flying towards you with the pin still in its body.'

Nick shook his head and tugged at his unshaven cheek with his fingers.

It was then that I realised we were not alone. Someone else was in the apartment. Listening in the hallway. From Nick's open-plan kitchen I saw her. A short woman with long black hair, dressed in pyjamas, walked towards me with my coat in her arms.

'So you are Tom Banbury-Mines.'

She threw the coat into my lap and said something to Nick in Greek. He shook his head and groaned.

'This is my sister, Elena.'

He stood up and disappeared into the bathroom. We could hear water begin to trickle from the shower.

Elena stood so close to me that I noticed her pyjamas were patterned with moons and suns. Rather childish for a woman in her thirties.

'I'll tell you something about my brother, ok?'

'Ok.'

'If Dad has earache, Nikos gets earache. If I've got bronchitis, Nikos gets bronchitis. If my mother cries, Nikos cries. So it's lucky that none of us are mad isn't it?'

She pointed to the door.

'I am looking after my brother, so you can go home. Shall I call you a cab, Mister Money Bags?'

Thanks to our agency's generous health insurance package, the hospital Nick ended up in looked more like a small castle for the rich and unstable than a lunatic ward. The Abbey even had a moat with two white swans that seemed permanently asleep as they drifted on the stagnant algae-covered water.

Two very attractive resident female doctors carried hypodermics between their fingers as if they were carrying cocktail cigarettes from one party guest to another. As I parked my Porsche in the almost empty car park, I wondered if the doctors had somehow tranquillised the swans in the same way they had tranquillised Nick. Large doses of colourless liquid were injected into his nervous system via the azure veins in both his arms. I liked to think the doctors filled their syringes from the water in the moat, which, like Lethe, the River of Forgetfulness, made their patients forget the troubles of their earthly life. I held Nick's hand in my hand and felt peaceful and calm for the first time in many years.

Unfortunately his sister was at his bedside too. Elena had to be polite to me because she knew The Abbey was better than an overheated institution with no windows. She sat on a chair on the right side of his bed and I on a chair on the left side of his bed. As Nick lay between us, moaning on two white pillows,

I came to think of his sister as a sort of guard dog. That is how she appeared in my dreams anyway, often with three heads, informing me that it was her duty to guard the sick. The doctors left me alone with Nick the few times his sister was absent, but one afternoon, when Elena brought him food his mother had cooked for him and stayed by his side to watch him eat it, he suddenly started to speak in a voice that was rather like my own.

'I am eight years old. The year Britain went decimal and John Lennon wrote 'Imagine'. The year *A Clockwork Orange* was released and I lost it with my father . . . '

'Nikos?' Elena murmured something in Greek and tried to clamp her hand over his mouth but he shrugged her away. His words were my words and I listened in a cognac-soaked trance.

'This is the year I run into the meadow. My Dutch governess is picking mushrooms on her knees. She says . . . "Ah, you have a knife in your hands. May I use it to cut the fungi?" I am shaking. She says, "How is your heartbeat today?"

'"My heartbeat is jumping all over the place, *danke*."

'She kisses my cheek and her kisses feel like a bite. A bite of love so startling I want to die in her milky arms. I want her to untie the white ribbon wrapped round the end of her plait and I want her golden hair to cover me like a shroud. She says: "One day I will take you to visit the Netherlands. In Holland we are nice to our children. Especially in Limburg, where my parents were born and where many mushrooms grow. Yes, I will take you to see the castle gardens at Arcen."'

Elena pleaded with me to stop him but I pretended not to notice. I had to fill Nick in. I wanted to give him more information. He would need to know how my Dutch tutor stood up in court wearing her white leather heels, holding the Bible in her soft hand as she told the jury in some detail (my fingers were in my ears) how my father beat me and how my mother looked the other way. I needed to feel through Nick whatever it is I felt then because I feel nothing now, but the two female doctors suddenly appeared and took over. They asked me to leave the room while they wrote notes in spidery black ink and clipped them to a file on the end of Nick's bed.

•

I drove home feeling more optimistic about the future than I can remember for a long while. When my mother rang my mobile to enquire about the weather, I parked in a lay-by and told her not to feel so bad about 'the events', as we called them. I even asked her if she recalled the name of the Dutch tutor she had employed to look after me all those years ago? I could imagine the colour draining from her face as she thought about this. After a long, tortured silence, she whispered, 'Cornelia. Yes, her name was Cornelia. She liked to collect mushrooms in the orchard. You called her Cokkie.'

I made a note to give Nick this new information. Cornelia was Cokkie. But I would have to get past his guard-dog sister first.

Elena did not usually come to the hospital on Wednesdays so I decided to make Wednesday my main visiting day. I would take Nick for a walk in the grounds and fill him in. When I arrived he was sitting in an armchair in his dressing gown watching a Laurel and Hardy film on TV. I noticed he was wearing his outdoor shoes rather than slippers and that his suit and a few magazines had disappeared from his locker. He waved to me cheerfully and asked if I'd mind getting him a cup of tea from the canteen.

'Of course,' I smiled. 'How about a couple of scones as well?' The canteen at The Abbey provided a homemade cream tea that I had shared many times with Nick. I even spread strawberry jam on his scone for him, as if he was a child.

The canteen appeared to be entirely deserted. A clock ticked loudly on the wall. As I made my way to the counter (longing for a cigarette) and searched for scones among the white plastic plates on which biscuits were paired with various fruits (two ginger-nuts with a wedge of orange, two bourbons with a slice of kiwi), I heard someone call my name.

'Thomas. Come and sit next to me.'

Elena had got to the canteen before me. In fact she had put her coat over two of the green leather armchairs in the far corner as if she were expecting me to arrive. She had even bought a pot of tea and two slices of cheesecake. I was forced to sit down with her, vaguely nervous to be alone with this enigmatic but stern sister. We chatted generally about Nick's recovery but that was obviously not what she wanted to talk to me about.

'Why are you so attached to my brother, Tom?'

Elena spooned the cherries off the cake and seemed more relaxed than usual.

'I don't really know.' I told her the truth. 'I just think your brother is an exceptional person.'

'You really smell of drink,' Elena leaned forward. 'You're a drunk, aren't you?'

'Yes, I'm a drunk.'

She closed her eyes as if trying to gather her thoughts. I noticed that her eyelids were dusted with pale blue eyeshadow that glittered and sparkled under the lights. When she opened her eyes again her manner was no longer amiable. I quickly understood that I was not out of my depth, it was just that Elena was swimming alongside me in the deep end.

'The doctors think my brother is having a nervous breakdown.'

I attempted to smile.

'Your brother is very sick.'

She leaned forward.

'*Yes. He's suffering for you.*'

Elena licked a few crumbs of cheesecake off her lips and gazed out of the window at a black Jaguar with tinted windows driving out of the car park. Its engine suddenly stalled near the poppies growing on the banks of the moat – and then started again with a jump. Even this did not wake the two sleeping swans adrift on the dark water.

Elena turned her gaze back to me.

'It's very difficult for my family. You see, Tom, I know my brother has a lot of empathy . . . but your kind of problems are not Nikos' kind of problems.'

'Yes,' I replied solemnly. 'I can appreciate that.'

'His kind of problems when he was a kid were having the electricity cut off because Dad couldn't pay the bills. He never had a Dutch tutor. He went to a comprehensive school off the Holloway Road.'

I poured myself another cup of Earl Grey, the tea my mother drinks alone in one of the twelve rooms of the family house she refuses to sell.

'Yes. I read his CV when I employed him, Elena.'

One of the female doctors walked into the canteen and lit a cigarette, despite the No Smoking sign displayed on the wall.

Dr Agnes Taylor had prescribed most of Nick's medication and overseen his occupational therapy. She waved at Elena with the bottle of mineral water she had just purchased.

'The taxi arrived. All fine.'

Elena nodded.

'I saw it go past, thank you.'

I felt unspeakably queasy at this exchange. The Jaguar pulling out of the driveway had made me shiver slightly. Did I imagine that Nick was waving to me from the other side of the tinted windows?

Dr Agnes Taylor glanced at me and smiled.

'How are you feeling today, Tom?'

'My heartbeat is very good today, thank you.'

'Your heartbeat? Well it's good that it's good, isn't it?'

Something was pressing down on my left wrist. I realised Dr Taylor had placed two of her fingers on my pulse, her perfume mingling with the sugar and cream of the cheesecake.

'A rest here at The Abbey will do you good, Mr Banbury.'

'Yes,' I replied, though in fact what I said was 'Ears'. Which is how men of my class say yes.

'Ears.'

For an hour after Elena left the canteen, my forehead was streaked with eczema, the twenty-four hour psychosomatic weather that can turn my face into a blazing sunset at any moment of the day.

•

Ah. Where am I? We will have to spin time forwards to where I am now.

How reassuring it is to sit on the edge of my own bed again. To sip an eggcup brimming with cognac and glimpse the London dawn. The car alarms that pierce the calm of the early morning are a relief after The Abbey's more panicked silence. The woman who owns the flower stall across the road is setting up for the day. She is bashing the stems of her lilies with a small hammer and placing them in silver buckets of water. It is now 6am and I'm too drunk to use a toothbrush. Too drunk to splash my face. I'll make my way to McDonald's on the High Street. Have you seen them, those men and women who sit on the red Formica chairs early in the morning? Eating their breakfast? No longer mad, but dazed instead. Medication has culled them. Chomping on the hash browns. Sucking up sweet strawberry shakes through the straw. Have you seen the expression in their eyes? The way the muscles in the face hang down to the floor? Don't be frightened. We are all of us breathing in atoms that were once forged in the furnace of a star. There are tiny shards of your life inside them and their life is inside you too. Do you know what they are saying to you?

They are saying good morning.

PILLOW TALK

'Why are people so thirsty at night?'

Ella, who is lying in Pavel's arms, sips her glass of iced water and listens to people putting money into the soft-drinks machine on the landing outside their hotel room. She can hear the tops of the cans being ripped off and then the strange intense silence of people drinking their first three gulps.

'Sometimes you get a choking feeling at night,' she replies 'It makes you want a drink nearby, just in case.'

'You don't feel like you're choking, do you?'

'No. I don't feel like I'm choking.' She kisses his fingers.

'Do you know, when I was a little girl, I was so light I could stand on my father's hand and he would lift me up to the ceiling?'

Pavel passes her his cigarette. Ducados. *Autentico Tabaco Negro*. A cheap Spanish cigarette they both like, especially after sex in a hotel bed made with clean cotton sheets and never enough blankets in spring.

Earlier, they had spent their last evening in Barcelona walking up and down the Ramblas, stopping to look at four grey rabbits for sale in a kiosk under the plane trees.

'Would you eat this rabbit?' Ella stroked the baby of the batch, rubbing her fingers against the soft strip of fur between its ears.

'Sure. I'm Czech. We're like the Chinese, we eat anything that moves.'

A tall North African man selling jewellery from an orange blanket on the pavement made shhp-shhp noises to get their attention, and then offered (in a low whisper) to sell them hashish. Ella bought a watch studded with rubies instead and told Pavel the time.

'It's nine o'clock. Let's eat.'

All around them people had finished work and were now sitting in cafes tucking into plates of meatballs, *calamares* and *tortilla*, wiping their hands on thin tissue napkins with *Gracias Por la Visita* printed in blue ink on every one.

'Why do people always say "I love you" in a sad voice?' Pavel smiles in the special way that shows his gold tooth.

'I've never understood why,' Ella replies.

Surname. Given names. Nationality. Date of birth. Sex. Place of birth. Date of issue. Date of expiry.

Pavel, who was born in what used to be called Czechoslovakia, has two passports. Ella, who was born in Jamaica but has lived in the UK since she was three years old, has a British passport. When the airport official, a man who is barely five foot tall and whose side parting is so straight it looks like it's been drawn on with a felt-tip, frowns at their documents, their hearts beat a little faster on the other side of the perspex barrier. What if he asks them to explain where they are from? What would they say? 'A bit from here, a bit from there.' Would this be enough information for the small guy whose bright eyes spin such a hostile glare over their faces? When the official finally nods and at last hands them back their passports, they walk straight into the Duty Free shop. Pavel wants to buy Ella the perfume he likes best. The one in the ribbed glass bottle that reminds him of old-fashioned European hotels with marble floors and red velvet sofas. Hotels that are dark rather than light, all the better for flirting with a stranger under crystal chandeliers, for sharing a bed that is home for a few nights only, a bed for sex rather than sleeping in. He hands over his credit card and tells the woman not to bother wrapping the perfume because he has twelve minutes to find his way to Gate 24. When Ella kisses him thank you, he knows it's a bitter, sweet kiss. Tomorrow he has an interview in Dublin with a firm of architects, and if he gets the job it means he will have to live far away from her.

Another airport. Another country. Another hotel.

Pavel turns left into a pub he knows well, just opposite Trinity College Dublin, and orders a pint of Guinness. The interview, he suspects, was a disaster. Every time he replied to a question asked by the

Japanese director of the firm, a man with gleaming black shoes on his tiny feet, Mr Kymoto lowered his eyes.

He searches for his cigarettes and finds the battered pack of Ducados. When he discovers there is only one broken cigarette inside it, a woman sitting alone at a nearby table offers him one of hers.

'Thank you.' Preoccupied with his failure to charm Mr Kymoto, he takes the cigarette without looking at her.

'Where are you from?'

'Český Krumlov.'

'Where?'

He glances first at the magazine she's reading and then at her face. Beauty is a shock to the nervous system, he thinks while she passes him her lighter, especially when he's not expecting it. Not expecting glass-green eyes and long chestnut hair piled on top of her head in the casual way he likes. She tells him she grew up in County Cork but now works in the box office of a theatre. It's great, she says, not too bad really, better to be on the phone all day in a theatre than an office; she gets to meet actors and to see all the shows for free. But she misses her friends. He must miss, um, what was it called, Český Krumlov, mustn't he? Pavel shrugs.

He knows that he offended the Japanese boss but he doesn't know why. Was it a major or minor offence? When he left the Czech Republic, the last exhibition he saw, before it was closed for reconstruction, was at the Police Museum. It was called Road and Traffic Offences. Some were minor and others major but he couldn't remember why.

In the morning, Pavel strokes his new lover's hair, his thin white legs wrapped around her freckled, fleshier legs. He glances at a photograph of a man pinned to her bedroom wall, a man who resembles himself, but is definitely someone else. There is something about the love beaming through the man's eyes that makes Pavel feel ashamed.

'Shall we go for a coffee in Grafton Street?'

'Don't you want breakfast?' She is tired and slow, taking her time to start the day.

He shakes his head. Sharing breakfast feels more intimate to him than making love to a stranger. Pavel wants to go straight to the airport but he doesn't know how to tell that to the woman with long curls and glass-green eyes.

'I'm going to miss my plane,' he says.

'Do you want to meet again?'

'Yes.' Pavel looks down at his bare feet. 'But, um, I've got a girlfriend in London.'

She smiles when he asks her for the number of a taxi company and suggests he call a helicopter instead. And then he realises he has spent all his euros and will not be able to pay the driver. He's only got an English twenty-pound note. The woman has turned her back on him and disappears into the kitchen to make coffee for herself. At the same time a message on his answerphone tells him that last night, Ella lost her front door keys. Her voice sounds stressed. 'I can't get into my house.'

'So you found your keys?' Pavel's voice is different. He sounds to Ella as if he is drowning.

'Someone else found them.'

'Where were they?'

'I dropped them in the bookshop.'

'Who gave them back to you?'

'That French man who works there. We discovered we were wearing identical shoes.'

'What kind of shoes?'

'Scottish dancing shoes.'

'I'm jealous.'

'But you had an affair in Dublin.'

Pavel says, 'I didn't mean to. I didn't set out to have an affair.'

Ella walks away. Probably, Pavel thinks, to the bookshop where the French man who wears the same shoes is waiting for her. He will suggest they take the Eurostar to Paris, straight to the Gare du Nord, and of course he will tell her that the best way to discover Paris is by walking the city in their identical Scottish shoes. He will show her the Parisian parks with their terraces and octagonal fountains and they will kiss under every tree and then he'll take her to a hotel in the Marais where she will punish Pavel by having the most exciting sex she's ever had in her life. In fact Ella rings him from work to tell him to pack his shirts and move out. And then his phone rings again. It is Mr Kymoto, calling from Dublin. He tells Pavel they liked his ideas, his qualifications were impeccable, but unfortunately they did not feel he had long-term loyalty to the firm.

'I'm not going to move out.'
    'I know you're not.'

Pavel is lying on his side of the bed and his girlfriend won't let him touch her. After a while Ella turns towards Pavel and pulls his ponytail, hard.

'You look fucking ridiculous.'

'I know.'

'Cut it off.'

'I can't.'

'I want you to be someone else.'

'Who do you want me to be?'

'I want you to be kind and wise. I want you to be a father who loves his children. I want you to be attentive to me and faithful for ever. I want you to always fancy me and respect and admire me and I want you to be older and more confident.'

'But I'm not,' Pavel says. 'I'm not a father. I'm not very wise.'

'I know.' Ella turns away from him.

Pavel's hands are not just white. They are the alabaster white of Catholic saints. Ella's father had wide, dark brown hands. But he was not wise. He left the house one night and never came back to tell her mother why. He left home to make another home and other children and then he left that home as well. Her father had many homes but no home.

He was not wise. Only in his hands. His hands were strong and in a way, they were wise. When he held her in his arms, she could feel his love for her. And when she was three years old she stood on his hands and he'd lift her up into the air until she touched the ceiling.

'Let's go for a walk.' Pavel risks kissing the back of her neck.

'We can walk by the Thames to that Portuguese place and have coffee.'

When Ella kneels down and ties the laces of her shoes, Pavel glares at them. It's quite unusual for a woman to own the same shoes as a man. Especially Scottish dancing shoes, men's dancing shoes with long laces that criss-cross up the shins. They walk on the paved bank of the Thames, cold and silent, listening to a busker play the bagpipes while two huge industrial barges sway on the oily churning water.

'Look, he's also got the same shoes as you!' Pavel points at the busker. He laughs now, squeezing Ella's hand. 'They must be very common, this kind of shoe.'

'Not really,' Ella replies, trying not to smile. 'It's not common for women to wear men's dancing shoes and to find a bookseller who wears them too. Specially as he's not Scottish and neither am I.'

They walk into the Portuguese cafe and kiss the owner's new baby, who was born last week and is now the star of the establishment.

'Good evening, your royal highness,' Pavel says when she is passed into his arms.

Later, when Pavel and Ella, now too tired to walk home, wait by the bus stop, he tells her he did not get the job in Dublin. The word 'Dublin' makes his girlfriend stiffen and move away from him. Pavel touches his throat. More than anything he wants a glass of water.

'Have you ever had that weird feeling in an airport when you panic and don't know what to do? One screen says Departures and another screen says Arrivals and for a moment you don't know which one you are. You think, am I an arrival or am I a departure?'

Ella is frowning, looking out for the bus.

'I don't know what you're saying.' Ella's voice is suddenly angry. 'Do you mean you don't know whether you're staying or leaving . . . is that what you're trying to say to me?'

'I'm sorry about Dublin,' Pavel murmurs into her hostile brown ear.

The bus arrives and they step inside, fumbling for change. Not knowing if everything is all right between them, they glance at the passengers in their scarves and hats and overcoats. Some of them are drinking fizzy cold drinks from cans. They hold the drink to their lips, eyes half shut, tense and concentrated as they gulp down the liquid, briefly stopping to catch their breath before lifting the can once more to their lips.

CAVE GIRL

My sister Cass thinks that ice cubes in the shape of hearts will change her life. Cass is a Stone Age girl. She hopes hearts will bring her love in the same way the Ancients thought dancing for the Gods would bring rain. She does the whole atmosphere business: turns off all the lights in the house and burns up a bargain pack of Tesco night-lights to make fake moonlight in her bedroom. After a while she makes herself what she calls a Piña Colada (some sort of milkshake), lies on the bed and sobs to a CD. It's hard to believe that that small silver disc can spin her to the other side and back. Cass wants to be somewhere else. She has been abducted by visions of paradise that are not here, and to punish me for being happy, she twisted her hair into a tight plait and cut the whole lot off. I used to be scared of open spaces until I realised it was indoors that was the most frightening.

At night the satellite dishes on the roofs and walls throw spectral shadows across the tamed gardens. I have grown to love the bronze doorknobs in the shape of jungle beasts: a lion's head, a tiger, a snake. These seem to me to be caveman icons on the doors of the bankers and dentists who live here, a way of keeping in touch with The Divine. Sometimes I lie flat out on the gravel under one of the new shrubs and feel the electricity charge me up. The TV repeats. The CD players and video hires, personal computers, microwaves, dishwashers and hairdryers. It gives me a thrill because I know the world is very old. At night, I sometimes hope that an Ancient will find me shivering in front of the TV eating Kentucky Fried Chicken. He will teach me how to sharpen flint and I won't know what to teach him because I don't know how to make antibiotics.

And then one night Cass told me her secret. Unburdened her confidence on my white-boy shoulders. She said she wants a sex change.

'What, into a man?'
'No, into a woman.'
'But you are a woman.'
'I want to be another kind of woman.'

'What does that mean, Cass?'

'I want to be light-hearted,' she begins, and already the worry lines on her forehead come into focus. 'I want to be airy.' My sister is whispering this to me under the new shrub in the dark. Her sad girl breath makes me dizzy. She says, 'I want to have blue eyes for a start, that's the trick. Blue eyes are the gentlest, sexiest, most ambivalent eyes. My blue eyes will cut out, but they will also be very much there.' When Cass says 'very much there', a thrill jolts through my stomach. She chews her nails for a while and then says, 'I want to be a pretend woman.'

I'm glad the gravel is clean and all the cats well fed here. I hate the way butchers display the insides of animals on silver trays.

Cass continues talking, her eyes shut tight and the light from the little lamp post chuffing over her shorn black hair. I've found a surgeon to do the op, she says in a flat voice. I can already see him drilling a hole in my sister's forehead with a rusty nail. I don't want to talk to her any more.

•

There's been a pile-up on the motorway nearby. A furniture van collided with a baker's truck. The drivers crawled out of their vehicles streaked in blood to find a load of chocolate éclairs and cream cakes splattered on leather sofas and office chairs. I don't want to see anything shocking ever again.

So this woman walks up the gravel drive, long legs, wearing sandals even though it's raining. Sandals with little heels and criss-cross straps over the instep. Dragging her bag with limp wrists, smiling under a dirty blond fringe, and the bluest eyes, kind of flat eyes, can't get inside 'em but she's got energy in her body and she says, 'Hi Bruv. Do you like my fake snake?' I don't know who she is or what she's talking about and then I see she's pointing to her fake snakeskin sandals.

'I'm Cass,' she smiles, dimpling her cheek.

Cass doesn't have dimples. And she never wears sandals with little spiky heels. And her hair's not blond.

There's something about this woman's voice, it just twinkles over me, cool and easygoing like a best friend in a great mood.

'Let's sit outside even though it's raining.' She smiles and takes out a wedge of Swiss cheese from her bag – sets about effortlessly slicing it, whooshing her fringe out of her eyes with her long fingers, nibbling at the cheese like she's got a bit of an appetite but doesn't want to hog the whole lot.

'I like Swiss cheese because of the holes,' she says airily, and then when she sees I'm freaked out her voice goes gentle and low.

'Hey, you'll get used to the new me. Don't look so frightened.'

She makes a shivering noise with her breath as we drag our chairs out into the garden, her little heels sinking into the grass, poking holes in the lawn, just like in the Swiss cheese.

'I like the rain.' She dimples again. 'No sun to damage our skin structure.'

When she speaks it's like she's trailing the tips of her fingers across the surface of a swimming pool, no gloomy silences or deep breaths before saying something truly hideous. And she smells of soap and deodorant. The old Cass never used deodorant. She used to say it was a trick to make her feel dirty so she would use something she didn't need. This Cass laughs with her eyes and she is all here, but she's also far away, admiring the rose bush like she's never seen it before, noticing there are bugs on the leaves and thinking aloud about how to spray them away. My sister would do something gross like eat the bugs rather than use a pesticide. This Cass leans back in her chair, dusts the crumbs of Swiss cheese off her white linen dress and suggests we plan some pleasure outings. Should we go to the cinema and see something light-hearted? What do I think? Cass never used to ask me what I think.

This is the unhappiest day of my life. I think I'm in love with my new sister. I want to find out who she is. I want to stare into her pretend blue eyes. I want to write my phone number across her hand and brag about her to my friends. I want to play with her hair and lift her onto my new bicycle and lie in the dark with her and show her my new computer game.

Something has just been massacred. There's a pile of bloody feathers on the gravel. A cat has caught Dickie, the neighbour's budgie, named after the famous cricket umpire. Dickie Bird's eyes have been gouged out and his head chewed up. His intestines are lying under the new rose bush.

•

I tell Cass what's on my mind because she seems
to want to know.

'Well . . . ' She bends her head to one side so
her long hair falls over her shoulder. 'See, you are
my brother and I am your sister.' Then she says,
'You'll find a girlfriend soon, and anyhow, why
don't we go inside and watch that stoopid sitcom
we like?'

When she stands up she yawns and her blond
eyebrows rise up on her forehead and then she
quickly puts her hand over her mouth and giggles.
There's a ring on her finger. A thin silver ring with
a heart and two baby doves welded onto it. And her
nails are clean with shiny see-thru pink stuff painted
on them. When my new sister looks at me, I feel I
am precious to her.

'Come on, Bruv. Let's go inside.'

I'm frightened to go inside and breathe all over the
wallpaper.

The man who does the TV weather for the
nation finished his forecast tonight by saying,
'Beware of the chill winds to come.'

Another thing. The ice in my Pepsi jumped out of the glass of its own accord.

I'm sick with longing for the new Cass. She has become airy, like she said she wanted to. For a start, she doesn't have opinions; she listens to what I have to say as if I am someone important. And when I tell her a joke she laughs, shining her dimples in my direction, making toast with lots of butter, just how I like it. When she eats toast, she breaks it up in the palm of her hand and kind of pecks the crumbs into her mouth, always on the lookout for something I might need. I take more care of how I look these days because I want her to think well of me. She particularly likes my trainers with red lights on the heels, the ones old Cass said made me look like a sad fuck.

'You're a style angel,' this Cass says, and then bends down to wipe off some cereal that's stuck itself to my shirt. She makes me want to do things for her too. Run her baths, put a new fuse in her hairdryer, walk to the shops and buy her chocolate bars and magazines. I'd cut off my arm if I thought it would please her. But I'm scared too. I'm fucking terrified. What if Cass morphs into her old self? What happened to it anyway? What if old Cass suddenly jumps through the smooth white skin of new Cass, laughing like a demon?

The men around here all make excuses to talk to her when they get back from work. I've noticed how they chat from inside their cars, air conditioning on and the windows down. Nothing makes sense any more. Cass leans in towards them, she is all there, light hearted and smiling, listening to how their day has been and how bored they are with their wives. Some of them give her presents.

Mr Tollington with the wart on his chin from Number Six gave her a tacky gold chain with a creamy pearl on the end – presented to her in a little box lined with red velvet. Cass smiled at him like he was the only man in the world. She even let him put it on for her, his horrible manly fingers lingering on her neck. Worst of all, Mr Lewenstein, who is quite good-looking I suppose (everyone knows he's got a mistress in Malta), gave her a bracelet plaited from three kinds of gold with a tiny padlock to snap it shut on her wrist. He had the lock engraved with the letter C, 'personalising it' he growled from his car window, a flash Jag that he pays me to wash for him on Sundays. Why does she bother talking to these men? I know she knows they're boring so what does she get out of it? Why does she care whether they like her or not?

'I told you,' she says, her voice sort of serious but flirtatious as well, 'I want to be a pretend woman. The surgeon did well. He really fiddled with my controls.'

She breathes out when she says this, like something amazing has happened to her. Where has the old Cass gone? Did the surgeon slop her into a stainless-steel tray?

I need an Ancient to find me now. We've got things to discuss and I know he could help me. He would have answers to where souls go after death and how people transform themselves from one thing to another. He made baskets woven from asparagus stalks and fires from frozen flints. He even knew about the sweat glands of poisonous frogs and which mushrooms were toxic. I want to ask him if he's scared of the dark and things lurking in the sea like I am, and if he ever had a sister who changed herself like Cass did.

Her blue eyes take me in, and freeze me out.

PLACING A CALL

You are telling me something I don't want to hear. You are telling me the honest truth. We are standing in the garden and it is dusk. There are rain clouds in the sky and midges and someone is planting a rose bush in the garden next door. The telephone is ringing.

The telephone is ringing. I run into the house and pick up the receiver. The telephone is pressed against my ear, someone is calling and I am answering. I am saying hello into hard black plastic but I hear the dial tone and the ring tone happening at the same time. Someone is missing. Someone is trying to get through. And then I remember there is a bird in the garden that imitates a telephone when it sings. I can see it now in the tree in the garden where you are telling me the honest truth. It is singing in an old-fashioned ring tone, it is singing like a land line. I run back into the garden.

We are standing in the garden and it's autumn and there's a bird in the tree that imitates a telephone when it sings. Your hair is silver but you are not old. Under your soft silver hair is your skull with your central nervous system inside it. It is dusk and it has started to rain. The roots of the eucalyptus tree that grows in the garden are spreading under the house. Our daughter is sleeping inside the house under a photograph of the sea. She is covered in a thick blanket. Her bed stands on a green carpet. There are two stains on the carpet.

You are wearing a white shirt and a suit and under your soft silver hair is your skull. While you speak the honest truth I am thinking about the time we ate horse steaks in Paris. The waiter served the dish of the day and the dish of the day was horse. It was like eating a unicorn in the twenty-first century. My iPod was playing a song we'd never heard before. You untangled the headphones and pressed them into your ears and you lifted my fingers and pressed them into your mouth.

But now we are standing in the garden and the telephone bird has stopped making calls no one answers. The car alarms and police sirens have stopped too. Silence is cruel in cities where missing people need to hide in noise. But we are standing in the garden in the rain and you have not stopped telling me the honest truth and I wonder if the telephone bird will one day learn to sing computer start-up sounds.

Your silver hair is wet. Our daughter is pretending to sleep inside the house under a photograph of the sea and she's listening to the rain which always makes sorrow bigger and hard things softer. I walk towards you, bumping into things on the way. Kissing you is like new paint and old pain. It is like coffee and car alarms and a dim stairway and a stain and it's like smoke. I am looking into your eyes and I can't get in. You have changed the locks and I have an old key that doesn't fit and our daughter is making her way across the garden towards us, holding her thick blanket. You are telling me you are dead, and I say yes, I know you are. We miss you and since you've gone I've forgotten all my pin numbers, I can't remember the code to my gym locker or where the honey is or where I put the blue pillowcase – and could you tell me, again, where exactly the sea is, in that photograph?

SIMON TEGALA'S
HEART IN 12 PARTS

1

Simon Tegala leaned his back against the wall of
the American Embassy and held her against him.
It was an electrical event. Small voltages spread
through their limbs. She said, Honey, that was a
test burn. She heard his heart sounds: lub dup
lub dup lub dup. She noted they were fifth in the
queue for visas. Naomi was the Newton of atomic
kissing; erotic radioactivity buzzed through her
blackberry lips. They had been told to produce proof
of identity in triplicate. Driving license, passport
and a household bill. Naomi would not let Simon
Tegala see the photograph in her passport. She
said, Stop looking for me. I am here standing next
to you listening to your heart sounds. He knew
that her lips were the only country he wanted
to be in.

2

Simon Tegala decided to throw the I Ching to discover if Naomi loved him. At that moment the phone rang. While his father's voice disappeared into his answering machine Naomi walked into his apartment carrying something for supper wrapped in wax paper. When she asked him why he was so quiet and what he was thinking about, he said SHAKING. My father has Parkinson's disease. They salted the chicken and cooked it in its own sweet juices while the phone rang again. His father's voice said AMERICA and then it said DID YOU GET YOUR VISA and then he said other words which upset Simon Tegala. DON'T LIVE FAR AWAY. Naomi pointed to a red felt hat that hung on the coat hook in Simon Tegala's kitchen. He told her it was a fez and she told him it was a chechia. What is a chechia, her boyfriend wanted to know. It's a fez, she replied. And then she said, shall we go and visit your father and take him a cake?

3

Later, Naomi said to Simon Tegala, I want you to touch my body in the following order:

3. My ear

5. My belly

Simon Tegala's heart is a biomachine beating hard and fast as he searches for the missing numbers.

4

Mr Tegala is sitting in a cafe drinking a mug of tea thinking about how his father shakes and jerks his head and arms. Images of projected futures whir like a science fiction behind his eyes. He decides he wants to spend Christmas Day with her but fears she might think he's getting ahead of himself because it's only July. And anyway, he hardly knows her.

5

Naomi said, What do you mean you hardly know me? Simon Tegala stretched out his arm and tickled the nape of her neck where a curl had escaped from her hair clip. Tell me about your mother your father your brothers and sisters, Naomi. Look, Simon Tegala, his girlfriend replied, the past is a place I have left behind. I want to arrive somewhere else. How am

I going to get there if I hang out with a cyclist who has no car to run his girlfriend or his ageing father around town?

6

While he negotiated with the car salesman, it occurred to Simon that this man had a substantial volume of blood pumping through a purple vein on his forehead. The salesman (who wore a thick gold wedding ring on his finger) was pointing at the vintage Cadillac of Simon Tegala's dreams. Mr Tegala the customer had suddenly become butcher. He saw the salesman merely as a sum of parts with blood flowing between, through and around them. A biological highway of organs, venules and veins. The salesman, unaware that he was perceived merely in terms of circulation of the blood and lymph, smiled and said he'd make a friendly price for Mr Tegala. As they walked over to his office to complete the deal, the salesman twisted the band of gold round and round his knuckle.

7

When Simon Tegala said to Naomi, Perhaps we can talk about Christmas Day, she gazed out of the window of his new old Cadillac and pointed to a white cat sitting on a wall.

8

Mr Tegala plays back three messages from his father on his answering machine and decides to drive to a late-night movie on his own.

9

The usherette shone her torch on a red velvet seat and sat Simon Tegala next to a woman eating an ice cream in a cone. Halfway through the movie, the woman told Simon Tegala that her name was Caroline Joseph. At that same moment the plot took a twist. Simon Tegala had missed a crucial clue and the film made no sense from then on. On the screen a man swam in a pool of salt water. A woman in a bikini waved to him from a rock. Simon Tegala sneaked a look at Caroline Joseph. Her eyes were like spark plugs shining in the dark. She was all sharp edges, lathed and polished. So very different from Naomi. The film had a happy ending. When Caroline Joseph put on a jacket with a fake ermine-trimmed hood, Simon Tegala found himself saying, 'I've just bought a new Cadillac. Do you want a ride home?' Caroline Joseph was so perfect she looked like she'd just stepped off the production line of a factory in Germany. He unlocked the door of his new old Cadillac and she eased herself in, admiring the white leather seats and the way he gripped the steering wheel. She told him she lived in Hammersmith with her dog, a terrier called Bobby. Would he like to meet Bobby? Simon Tegala nodded enthusiastically. When he woke up next to Caroline Joseph the following morning she told him all about her family and he told her he was in love with Naomi.

10

Naomi said to Simon Tegala: It's over between us. I can't believe you wanted more sex magic because you think your father is dying. Simon Tegala's heart has two chambers: the upper chamber and the lower chamber. Blood flows between these chambers. Simon Tegala's heart is the size of his fist. What were you thinking, his ex-girlfriend shouts as she slams the door. Simon Tegala says, SHAKING. I was thinking about SHAKING.

11

This is his sixth day without Naomi. As Mr Tegala rides his bicycle to the pub, he hums his favourite Leonard Cohen song. A passing truck knocks him into the gutter. Simon Tegala is bleeding and bruised and he can't stand up. Apparently someone has called an ambulance. He wonders if Naomi would leave him if she knew Leonard Cohen was his hero. And then he remembers Naomi has left him anyway.

12

The nurse in Casualty asks Mr Tegala if he knows anyone who can drive him home. Simon Tegala winces because she is taking out the glass shards in his thigh with long silver tweezers. The nurse says, 'Now look up, because I'm going to put some antiseptic on your chin.' When he looks up he sees Naomi leaning against the wall, holding a brown paper bag full of apples. Look over there, Naomi says, and she points to the door. Simon Tegala sees his father waving at him with his right hand because his left hand is holding a steel crutch. His father is wearing a hat and an overcoat and he is speaking. The only person in the room who can understand him is Simon Tegala because his father can only whisper. We've come to get you son, the taxi is waiting outside. Next time keep your eyes open when you ride a bicycle. Naomi's red heels click across the floor towards Simon Tegala and then she is just one centimetre away from his lips.

ROMA

Her husband who is going to betray her is standing inside the city of Roma. She is talking to him over the wall because she is not invited inside. She says, 'You've broken my heart,' in the way an actress might say it. Standing by the fountain in the centre of Roma is the woman who admires her husband. She walks past him in jeans and trainers. Her neck and cheeks are flushed.

When she wakes up from this dream about her husband betraying her, the traitor is lying by her side. A radio in the room next door announces that the Federal Reserve has dropped interest rates in the USA and European markets are expected to follow suit. She puts her hand here and there on her husband's warm body and tells him nothing about her dream. In five hours they will be out of the British weather. They will spend four days in Portugal and then return to the UK for Christmas.

Their bags are packed. A cab will call for them. The lodger in the room next door, Mr Patel, the man who listens to the radio all day long, has bought her a present for the trip. A slab of Ayurvedic soap made from eighteen herbs.

It has been raining in Portugal for three days and nights. She walks down to the sea with her husband. The drenched succulents and rotting fishing boats have the same atmosphere of betrayal she experienced in her dream. She stares into the shallows of the salt lagoon. A stork stands in the mud.

And another.

Her husband takes a photograph of the two storks. When she holds his bag for him he comments on how pleasant her hands smell. She tells him it's the Ayurvedic soap that Mr Patel gave her and that he should try it too. That night they eat in the Cafe Emigrante. A shack restaurant in the poorer part of the village. Varnished bamboo poles line the crumbling walls inside. The cook throws bloody fish onto smouldering charcoal. They break bread, scoop up white cheese and shrivelled, sour olives. Outside it is raining again. Their hotel room is not a place that invites intimacy. The cold marble floor. The thin blankets that are not warm enough for December in the Algarve. Two single beds pushed together. She finds Roma once again in her dreams and it is a warmer place to be.

The river is full of stars in Roma. Baroque water flows over rocks and stones. Her husband who is going to betray her sits at a table with his admirer eating almond Easter cakes, iced white in the shape of small bells. His admirer is strong. Desire has made her strong. Her skin is tanned. Her eyes and hair are black. She shakes the three green bracelets on her wrists and says, 'I have thought about what you have to say and it's interesting.' His wife watches from the other side of the wall. 'He is in love,' she thinks. She knows he is trying not to be in love.

In the morning they dip sweet sponge cakes into milky coffee in the Cafe Emigrante. The siren from the factory on the other side of the river calls people to work. Women run out of houses clutching carrier bags and sandwiches wrapped in wax paper. This reminds her of the paper the Ayurvedic soap was wrapped in. The letters carved into the green soap told her it was called M-e-d-i-m-i-x and it was made in a factory in Chennai.

Returning to London. The same old bus routes. The dirty old roads. The Christmas trees glimpsed through windows of London houses. Blue lights glowing through the pine needles. She looks down at a scrap of paper in her hand. It tells her to buy a turkey. She invites Mr Patel to join them for Christmas lunch. Again he tells her how much he is enjoying his stay in the United Kingdom. There are no mosquitoes, no humidity, less pollution.

It is snowing.

It never snows in Roma. It is August in her dream. Romans leave their stifling city. They pack their bags and make off to the coast and mountains to swim in lakes and recover from the knocks and disappointments of the year. She sees her husband waiting for his admirer at a cafe that is closed for summer. The shutters are down. The tables and chairs stacked up. His wife knows what she must say to her husband from the other side of the wall. She says, 'You totally enriched my life.' His face is impassive but he cries. Tears fall from his eyes and arrange themselves on his cheek like Man Ray tears.

On Christmas Day she kisses her sleeping husband and opens the window. The radio in the next room describes the current peace talks, an American initiative in the Middle East. As they open their presents in bed, her husband wishes her a happy Christmas but she interrupts him. She says she knows he wants to leave her. She says she has noticed he has not unpacked his bags from Portugal.

She says she understands he is in love with someone else but does he think there is a chance they might make it through the coming year? He tells her this is true and he doesn't know what to do and he was waiting to tell her but he could not find the words. She does not tell him that she has been standing outside the city of Roma, watching and talking to him over the wall.

A BETTER WAY TO LIVE

My mother died when I was twelve years old. I watched her green eyes close, and then, for five shocking seconds, open again. When she closed her eyes for the last time, I was both relieved and devastated. My mother was a historian. When she died, everything she knew about the twentieth century died with her. As a child she told me stories I thought she'd made up. Later, I learned that the things she described had really happened in the world.

The Fall of the British Empire I associate with brown shoe polish and Mom's high heels, while Fidel Castro's army taking power in Cuba is irrevocably linked with the warm maple syrup she poured onto pancakes on Sunday mornings. My mother wanted a better life for Russian women selling their slippers in the Moscow snow and she wanted a better life for me, her London boy with bright eyes just like hers. I never once missed my father. He walked out on both of us before I was born and I hope he walked straight into a wall. When my school friends asked who my dad was I said Humphrey Bogart, because Mom and I watched *Casablanca* every Christmas and I thought he was the most handsome man in the world.

Although there have been times I've hated my life, there is no part of my city that I dislike. London for me is like surfing a grey wave in the rain. I even like the cracks in the paving stones. Ok, sometimes I yearn to be elsewhere. To live on a palm-lined drive in Florida, sunning myself at the edge of one of California's blue pools, singing moody tunes out into the American sunset. The Pacific rolling and everything in a petroleum haze. Don't think I have not dreamed of cruising America's tremendous steaming tarmac in a chrome machine, waving at bronzed brunettes in bikinis and chains of gold hugging their tiny waists. But my heart is in London with its tough tender girls walking arm-in-arm in their raincoats, smiling with teeth crooked, pierced eyebrows and lips, imperfect dreamers and schemers, loud laughers, yearners with highlights in their hair. Some of them have even yearned for me, but it is Elisa who grabbed my broken heart and understood that to lose your mother is to lose half your life. I had no father so it felt as though I had lost all my life. But Mom taught me something wonderful. She said, Be sure to enjoy language, experiment with ways of talking, be exuberant even when you don't feel like it because language can make your world a better place to live.

Elisa has just gone off to swap coats with her pal – something suede for something leather, always on the lookout for clothes that will kill her. I feel the same about music. I want to be killed by music; I don't want music to relax to, I want it to match the grief inside me, the years of weeping in overheated children's homes as a boy. Beethoven can get there sometimes. But enough of all this, something is going to happen. I want the world to know that I am going to prune the small bay tree in the garden and marry Elisa. We will throw a summer party in our garden and plant a lawn, lush and green from the April city rain.

'Elisa?'
　　'Yes, Joe?'

'Do you think there is a better way to live than this?'

'Oh yes. There must be.'

I used to ask the same question of the fat, cross-eyed carers who looked after me in the institutions that became my home after Mom died. They stuffed their mouths all day with stale pink sponge cakes that a local bakery donated to the 'orphans', and hit us when we wet our beds or asked questions that were beyond the limits of their minds. Every time they beat me, I chanted a phrase over and over in my head – beautiful breath   beautiful breath   beautiful breath – and as my mother had predicted, it made things better. Beautiful breath was Elisa, the teen-age girl in the dorm across the corridor. Elisa had a secret. At night she crept out of bed and stuck the coloured feathers she had plucked from a duster onto her grey-soled shoes with flour and water.

From the very first moment I saw Elisa, I knew we were destined to marry. The clips she put in her hair made my heart roar. Two green plastic butter-flies. They told me she wanted a better way to live, long before she stuck feathers on her shoes.

•

We dug the soil to sow the grass and now our three cats have paws soaked with mud and everywhere inside the house, on carpets and chairs, are cat-paw prints like fossils you find on rocky beaches. Elisa and I have lived through our own personal ecstasies and catastrophes. When we laze on the old kilim rug my mother bought from somewhere in Persia, our bodies are hesitant and love soaked. The moon is oily, the trees swollen with black blossom against the chemical sky. Although our interior worlds are volcanic, exotic, troubled, the everyday is beautifully predictable. We eat pancakes on Sundays – something I like to cook for Elisa, who secretly prefers toast and Marmite – we read the world press on our screens and Skype our friends. After breakfast we get dressed and browse in flea markets or walk by the river near the luxury flats that used to be warehouses or sit in city parks on benches that dead people have donated to the public. Our favourite inscription reads, 'I love you Joan from tiny George.'

We made the date for our wedding and carved it into the bark of our bay tree. Elisa whitewashed the wall at the back of the yard and her best friend, Rona, said it looked like a postcard she once saw of a fisherman's cottage in Greece. Rona rolled up her sleeves and made a soup with one hundred potatoes, sixty cloves of garlic and forty-seven leeks. Rona is very precise about everything. When Elisa asks Rona if there is a better way to live than this, Rona replies, You will have to be more specific about what you regard as 'this' and what you regard as 'that'. While Rona chopped her eighty-third potato into six slices, I made ten tall jugs of margarita and Elisa barbecued plenty of chicken drumsticks over an old oil drum sawed in half. Then we went off to dress for our Big Day.

As I soaked in the bath, I saw a starling through the window, swaying to and fro on the bay tree. Once again, the sad grey childhood shoes my bride decorated with feathers flashed before my eyes, as they have done so often in my adult life. And then I dragged in a vision for a wedding outfit. Yes, while men and women argue on the moon, I will go for the exuberant and baroque. I will swank around my Victorian house with its boarded-up fireplaces and nineteenth-century plumbing in a suit made from tartan and silk. I will comb my black hair already threaded with silver and scent it with rose water from the orchards of Istanbul.

•

My first glimpse of Elisa was through a haze of smoke from the barbecue. My orphan bride wore a silver mesh dress, lime sandals and yards of eyelashes. Beautiful breath   beautiful breath   beautiful breath. I loved every part of her. The registrar from Orpington looked us in the eye and said words like Honour and Cherish without blinking. Gnats hovered above the sizzling chicken. Pete and Mike exchanged a lustful look. A car alarm went off.

Elisa said Yes and I said Yes.

We said Yes in all the European languages. Yes. We said yes we said yes, yes to vague but powerful things, we said yes to hope which has to be vague, we said yes to love which is always blind, we smiled and said yes without blinking. I wished my mother could hear us say yes and I thought about the stories she told me when I was a child and walked on garden walls that seemed so high but she always said yes, yes climb up and walk on that wall, I will hold your hand and tell you about the skyscrapers of Chicago.

Elisa and I exchanged rings. The best man and best woman threw rice over our heads. We kissed.

We felt each other panic under our wedding clothes as the rice fell to the ground. Perhaps it frightened the starling because it flew away. It had some feathers missing from its neck and one of its eyes had closed up. We were pleased the bird had spotted somewhere better to live but we secretly wanted it to stay. And then we saw that our three cats were hiding in the bay tree and realised it had found a safer place to live.

Elisa and I, the last two smokers on earth, sit under the bay tree, listening to our cats purr while they sharpen their claws and lick each other clean. My new wife plays with my fingers and the sun, which is setting, prints colour into the concrete towerblocks.

Elisa says, 'Now that we are married, your mother is my mother too.' Yes, we are orphans groping for things we are connected to, vague and blind things like the cold bright wedding rings on our fingers. While I sit smoking with Elisa, a halo of midges circling her head as she crosses and uncrosses her long legs, I recall for her my mother's stories which sometimes sound like dreams: Benito Mussolini smiling in a hat with an eagle on it, the Wall Street Crash, a woman staring at a boat in Hiroshima, the Minghetti cigars my father smoked, Elise Davis walking on a fifty-foot high wire holding an umbrella, Rosa Parks on a Montgomery bus in the USA the day the buses were no longer segregated, Algerians eating honey cake after they won independence from France, a teenage boy climbing over the Berlin Wall that separated capitalism from communism, a line from a play called *Ubu Roi*: 'WELL PERE UBU, ARE YOU CONTENT WITH YOUR LOT?', Mahatma Gandhi, the Black Panthers, Tom and Jerry, powdered eggs, miners digging deep in the earth for coal.

I press my lips against Elisa's eyelids and lead her to the honeymoon chamber where I have dimmed the lights and washed the linen. Although my body is stuffed with the gauze of information and the soul has gone out of fashion, I still use plants to heal my wounds and pains. I put calendula ointments on my shins when I fall over and sip chamomile tea when I'm in shock, a flower the Egyptians dedicated to their gods. One day, when Elisa and I are long buried and have turned to dust, I hope a robot boy will find this document and correct my spelling mistakes with his silver fingers. Although he will look nothing like me, he too will be a son without a mother, his eyes open all night long.

A NOTE ON THE AUTHOR

Deborah Levy writes fiction, plays, and poetry. Her work has been staged by the Royal Shakespeare Company and widely broadcast on the BBC, including her dramatizations of two of Freud's most iconic case histories, *Dora* and *The Wolfman*. The author of highly praised novels including the Man Booker Prize–shortlisted *Swimming Home*, *Beautiful Mutants*, *Swallowing Geography*, and *Billy and Girl*, she lives in London.